In the chapter titled Dwyn, there is depiction of rape. While it is an important part of her story, as it is part of many of our stories, please take care reading and know you are not alone.

BANSHEE

BANSHEE

MAGGIE CRITCHLEY

For women everywhere who had to wait longer than most to find your people, its worth the wait and, so are you.

"To have no yesterday, and no to-morrow.
To forget time, to forget life,
to be at peace." -Oscar Wilde

Your death day is as much a surprise to you as the day you are born and, just like a birthday, it is cause for celebration. Someone who cares for you organizes, prepares, and waits for your arrival. They take care to usher you into the next phase of existence with reverence and joy. These ushers go by many names;here, they are called Banshee and their wailing is not a warning but a welcome.

Pronunciation Guide

This book may be short but some of the names are long or nuanced and are definitely Celtic in origin. Below is a guide to some of those tricky tongue twisters.

Realta : Rey-all-tuh
Siobhan : Shiv-awn
Dwyn: D-win
Oona : Uw-naa
Seren : Seh-run

CHAPTER 1

Happy Death Day

I was floating in nothingness, at least it felt like floating. No longer on fire, wherever this was it was so endlessly comfortable I wondered why people feared death so vehemently. Somehow aware, I found myself being guided in my floating by what I had inferred was some sort of current. Light slowly crept in with each passing moment a warm voice enveloped me. Aware now of being pulled, not forcefully, at a pace akin to my mother when going to market.

The voice came again. "Siobhan," it said softly. I knew without knowing that this was my name. The voice said it again, louder, as though trying to wake someone from a dream. Had it all been a dream?

Opening them slowly, my eyes peeled apart, I didn't want to pull my eyelashes; did I still have eyelashes? The room was so bright my eyes snapped shut reflexively. I breathed the cool sweet air deeply, hadn't my lungs burned away? One more deep inhale, one deep exhale. I opened my eyes more slowly

"No. We don't keep looking glasses because they can be used to travel Elsewhere and allow access here, we learned that the hard way," Realta explained.

"Alright, can you please help me with all this hair then," I asked politely. My new locks were thicker and more unruly than those I had previously, they were also the color of milk thistle which would have been shocking had I not become recently deceased.

During my pondering, Realta had gone and come back with a pile of what could only be assumed were garments, for which I was grateful. Realta handed them over with a nod and headed back out of the room.

Privacy. A thing I had not the benefit of in a very long time. Breathing deeply, standing as slowly as possible, lest I fall, the sweet smell of orange and cinnamon clung to my garments, which were clean and dry and for that I was once again, grateful.

The effort of clothing myself had exhausted my body, yet my mind kept racing with questions I wasn't sure had answers or if they did, anyone to answer them. Sitting back down on the bed as gently as spent muscles would allow, I focused on breathing to steady my mind. The one thought that persisted was "am I to remain alone?"

Realta swept back into the room then, as though in response to the silent query, bringing along with her a gaggle of Banshee.

"We're called a curse," Realta chuckled slightly, "a gathering of Banshee is called A Curse."

"Was I narrating again," my embarrassment would have blushed my cheeks had I any blood.

"No, it's just a fun little fact about us," Realta reassured.

"Macabre though our job may be, we do like to find levity where we can," another of the Banshee said.

"Levity," I scoffed, "I'm sure I don't know her."

The Banshee who last spoke gave a barking laugh at the jest.

"Very good," she smiled, which one only knew by the crinkle at the corners of her eyes, "I am Oona, glad to have ya."

Thus began the rest of The Curse introducing themselves, offering cheer where Siobhan had resigned to being lonely.

Oona, whose skin carried a pearlescent sheen, had grey eyes and hair was closer to magenta than the shades of purple that she and the others seemed to have.

"No one knows why," Oona offered with a shrug, "just lucky I guess."

"You will be sharing a room with Oona," Realta explained as they walked down a hallway toward Banshee living quarters, "and yours is across from Seren and Dwyn. You will not be going out on your own for quite a while and will go on any call any of them is sent out to, given you are not already busy. There is plenty to learn and you've got those spongy new brains with which to absorb it all. Your fellow Banshee are all happy to have a new addition."

At that, Realta stopped in front of a wider and taller doorway than I was used to passing through, in which a beautifully furnished and pristine room could be seen. Stone floor polished to such a gleam it appeared to be a glassy lake top. Crisp linen bedding in complementary shades of grey and purple, pillows so fat and fluffed I could hardly wait to use them.

A wardrobe stood against the same wall the doorway had been cut into, a large desk split the room down the middle and the window stood opposite the doorway. Twilight poured through the glass panes, washing everything in a soft pink light.

"It's always twilight," Oona whispered, not wishing to disturb their new cohort's awe, "it always feels like a dreamy late summer evening, there's always tea and scones and someone to sit with."

"Why are we all so afraid of death, if this is what happens after," I asked, sadness misting my eyes.

"This isn't what happens for everyone," Seren replied, "this is what happens to those of us who remained steadfastly precocious while alive."

"We are truly blessed," Dwyn said.

"Blessed be," the others responded in unison.

"Do you remember it," escaped my mouth before good sense could be found, "how you died?"

They each paused for a moment to consider who should go first, Dwyn volunteered.

CHAPTER 2

Dwyn

She had left her father's abuse and found that she could, in fact, make it on her own, though it was uncomfortable at first. Being a woman of privilege, she embarrassed herself on too many occasions to count with her ineptitude at caring for herself or how the world worked outside the gilded walls she had been raised within.

She preferred the company of women, a fact her father could not beat out of her, not for lack of trying. Dwyn rented a room at a boarding house intended for merchants and craftsmen, those who did not or could not sleep in their shops. Dwyn was the first prostitute in the house though, she certainly would not be the last.

Her first night on the street was uneventful, no one dared look at her never mind proposition. Two nights past, then four, then a week and she started to worry she would fail. One evening she ventured out yet again and this time a familiar face was waiting by the doorway as she made her way into the night.

"You're dressed too well," the man said.

He was tall, dark haired and well dressed. He could have been any man in the city coming to blow off steam.

"I beg your pardon," Dwyn stepped back into the doorway.

"The men will think you are just lost or waiting for your husband," he said, shaking his match to put out the flame he just struck to light his pipe, "or that police are using you as bait."

"These are the only clothes I have," Dwyn lamented.

"I am assuming there is at least one maid who works at this establishment?"

"Yes," Dwyn nodded.

"Ask her which dress maker in the city your lady of the house sees. Take some of your finer things to trade and have the dress maker tailor a handful of dresses meant for a Sunday lunch," he inhaled his tobacco deeply, exhaling in equal measure, "find a cheaper perfume that you can wear on nights you work. Use a heavier hand when you rouge and kohl."

"Why are you helping me?"

"Let's just say I appreciate an entrepreneurial spirit when I see it," he winked. She noticed just how handsome he was for the first time.

"Thank you," Dwyn nodded, "how can I repay the favor?"

"Not necessary, just keep yourself safe."

Dwyn turned to go back inside and when she looked over her shoulder, the man was gone without trace. The next morning, she did as instructed and inquired with the maid about a dressmaker.

The night she went out in her Sunday almost best, Dwyn met another Lady of the Night who became her companion while they worked. Her reputation grew within weeks and she was well on her way to being a well paid bang tail within two months. Dwyn kept only one rule when it came to deeds she was willing to perform, full on blanket hornpipe was right out. She used the excuse of keeping her virtue intact so that someday she may marry and her husband would be none the wiser.

Most men who purchased her company never pushed that boundary, those who did were squeezed within an inch of losing their prized appendage. The maid who helped her early on remembered how she liked her tea, ensuring it was at her bedside along with bread and fruit each morning after work, no matter the time she made it through the door.

Hydref looked every inch the season for which she was named and had been waiting for the kettle to heat when Dwyn happened upon her; humming to herself, hair not yet plaited, sunset curls spilling halfway down her back, uniform midway to being buttoned. Dwyn shut the door louder than she typically would have, announcing her presence so as not to startle the maid.

"Bore da," Hydref greeted her, hurriedly buttoning her collar.

"Gadewch i mi helpu," Dwyn snapped the last button into place.

"Diolch yn fawr iawn," she responded, making eye contact for the first time.

Dwyn was stricken by the depth of color she found there, soil in which she would find the most steadfast affection she would ever know.

"Hyfryd," Dwyn whispered.

"Hydref," she said, "fy enw i yw Hydref."

"Gwn," Dwyn corrected, tucking an errant curl behind Hydref's ear, "ac rydych chi'n hyfryd."

"We should not speak our native tongue where anyone can hear," Hydref turned to take the kettle off the stove.

"True enough," Dwyn lingered a moment longer before heading up to wash before bed.

When she finally felt clean enough, as clean as tepid water and Hudson's soap powder could help one feel, she oiled her body, slipped into her sleep clothes and made her way as quietly as possible to her room. A note had been set upon one of her pillows.

Same time tomorrow? I will have tea ready.

She knew without knowing that it was from Hydref.

They met the next morning and every morning after, always at the witching hour, always for tea, within a fortnight they had fallen deeply in love.

Dressed in their Sunday best, they made their way to Munday's for lunch.

"Do you enjoy what you do for work," Hydref asked after they had ordered their food.

"I enjoy that it pays well and that I have my own money," Dwyn answered flatly.

"What would you do instead, if you could?"

"Telegraphist sounds nice," Dwyn admitted, smiling brightly.

"Telegraphist," Hydref's laugh a ringing of bells throughout the pub.

"Yes," Dwyn chuckled, "I quite like the idea of passing along necessary information, being the first to know a secret."

"Being able to keep a secret is certainly important in your profession," Hydref sipped the wine that had finally been delivered.

"What about you," Dwyn asked around a bite of cheese, "what would you like to do instead?"

"I would own a bakery and make the prettiest pies around," she smiled broadly at the thought.

"You already keep baker's hours as it is and you do make a very good cup of tea," Dwyn encouraged.

They ate and drank in silence, enjoying their fare and taking in each other's company as earnestly as they could.

"I've a secret for you," Hydref dabbed at her mouth though she was the neatest eater Dwyn had yet known, "though you would be the second to know."

"Ah," Dwyn feigned disappointment, "second to know is better than not knowing at all, I suppose."

Looking around conspiratorially, Hydref drank down the last of her wine and whispered "Dw i'n dy garu di."

Dwyn shoved what was left on the plate in her mouth, washed it down with the remainder of her wine and asked "Are you ready then?"

A puzzled looking Hydref rose slowly from her chair, adjusting her gloves and hat without looking at Dwyn and followed her out in silence. As they passed a seldom used alleyway, Dwyn pulled Hydref into it, covering her mouth when she tried to protest. There, as the light of day was settling into twilight, Dwyn looked up into Hydref's concerned face and said "I love you too."

Hydref pushed Dwyn's hand away from her mouth, bending down the short distance between them, gently putting her lips to Dwyn's. Each relaxing into the touch as tension began building everywhere else. Dwyn grazed a thumb across Hydref's cheekbone, Hydref kissing the palm of her hand as she did. Running her fingers gently up Hydref's neck, pulling her closer along the way, parting their lips with the tip of her tongue.

Hydref responded passionately, biting Dwyn's bottom lip sharply, ensuring there was no telling where one of them ended and the other began. Hydref kissed her way down Dwyn's neck, making quick work of the buttons keeping her lover's body from her. A loving bite at Dwyn's collarbone elicited a gasp of pleasure, encouraging Hydref to stay the course she was on, loosening ribbons as she went. Not to be outdone, Dwyn's nimble fingers kept pace, exposing Hydref's presently goosed flesh, cupping a perfect handful of bosom. They stopped only when each had her fill of the other.

Smiling broadly, they helped each other with buttons and ensured neither had a hair out of place before strolling home arm in arm, as ladies do, blissfully unaware they had been seen.

The city on a Saturday night was brighter, louder and hotter than most other nights in the city. Everyone from Dock workers and ne'er do wells to the well off teemed about the dirty streets, ready to spend money on anything that would ease the burden of existing.

She and another of the many soiled doves, none more than seven and ten, took advantage of those needing to alleviate their aches, stood against the streetlamp, having just been lit, the gas fumes made their eyes water. It was the safest spot for displaying themselves, as such they had to get there early or miss out and wander the street peddling their wares. On its surface, the night seemed no different than any other Saturday and yet, something felt amiss. Everyone was a bit too shiny eyed, frenzy humming just beneath their skin as they set upon the city. Work weeks were stressful even for those in the easiest of professions, those who had laborious jobs were brutal at best so, letting off steam was taken very seriously.

They rounded the corner, kissing as they went, when Dwyn opened her eyes she found herself in her preferred dimly lit alley occupied by more than her preferred number of partners.

"Gentlemen," panic raised her voice an octave higher than she usually spoke, "while I would love to entertain all of you, only one has paid for my pleasure this evening and watching is not an available option."

The man who had just been kissing her, grabbed her forcefully by the neck, placing his free hand over her mouth to stifle her subsequent scream. Two men moved to block the entrance of the alley, a fourth and fifth swapped places with the first, shoved Dwyn to the ground. Dwyn tried her hardest to think of anything other than where she was, one of her assailants took notice and slapped her hard in the face to bring her back.

They went through multiple rounds of this, each time she felt herself floating away on a memory of a warm holiday, she was slapped back to the present. The man who had paid took his turn first, entering so roughly she was sure she was being ripped apart. Hot tears made their way down her cheeks, slicking the gloved hand covering her mouth, causing the man to whom it belonged to push down harder lest his hand slip and free her scream. He finished as quickly as he usually did, shoving out of her in disgust.

After tidying himself he swapped places with one of the men guarding the alleyway, who picked up where the first left off and so it went until they had all had a piece of her. When the last one, the one who had taken to slapping her, crawled on top of her, he did not push into her the way the others had. Keeping his hand over her mouth, he kissed her forehead before pulling his face just far enough away from hers.

A smile that showed too many teeth distracted her from the glimmer of cold iron he pulled from his pocket and shoved into her throat.

"You refused me week after week," he whispered as blood sprayed across both of their face, "I just wanted your company. I know what you are, and your lover is next."

Dwyn tried screaming but all that came out was gurgling blood as her body spasmed violently toward lifelessness. They stayed long after the light had faded from her eyes then popped off to the pub as though they hadn't just taken a dove from her nest.

"Then I woke up here," Dwyn smiled sadly, shrugging off latent emotion.

"Dwyn has always been one of our best," Realta offered, breaking the tension before heading to her office.

"Hydref sounds lovely," Siobhan said.

"She was," Dwyn studied the contents of her teacup, "she was kind, cared deeply about others and wrote the filthiest poetry I've ever read."

CHAPTER 3

Oona

After a break to bake more scones, it was Oona's turn. Even though her story was new to me, she relayed it with fervor most reserved for first tellings.

The Big Apple midwinter was lovely even if food was sometimes scarce. And no self respecting New Yorker calls it the Big fucking Apple, although it must be true that if you can make it here, you can make it anywhere. The Holidays with various Gods being celebrated, peoples and traditions will make you weak in the knees if you're doing it right. The whole building feels like one big family, hand me down recipes gifted away, voices raised in languages of neighbors, languages of love, peace and joyful new beginnings as the year comes to an end.

We never went hungry, dad made sure mom had whatever she needed to keep us nourished, but some days lunch was just plantains and beans. Dad moved to Washington Heights with his parents in the 50's or, as he puts it, "was moved," since he was only a toddler at the time. My parents met in 1965 when mom's family moved there from Biloxi and to hear them tell it, it was love at first sight. They married within a few months, my brother arrived within a couple of years and I within a year behind him. Manhattan was an ever evolving beast, but The Heights had always felt safe.

Nothing feels the way the city feels: bright, frenetic, ambition incarnate. The familiar smells and sounds of our old building played like a movie across the window I stared out of as we made our journey. Afrocentric beats from the family in 12F mingled with the garam masala prepped by the family in 12D while one of the kids who lived in 14G practiced his monologue for community theatre out of the stairs. In 14C, they baked the most delicious sourdough every week for anyone who wanted some and 14B made vegan butter that's so good it'll make you think you've gone to heaven.

Our community offering was mom. Her nimble fingers wove the best braids within five blocks, certainly the best in the building. And so we would not snap, Dad decided we had to move to Long Island to live with family for a bit. The only reason I agreed to go was that it was still technically New York. I'd rather have been homeless than move to New Jersey. Even still, I felt my dreams littered along the highway in our wake as we drove along Route 27.

Nothing prepared any of us for the government pumping crack into our neighborhoods. It snatched souls, leaving husks where vibrant young men once stood. Turned stomachs at the sight of baking soda, ripped families apart and they blamed us, saying we created it but only one class of men seeks to destroy.

Closing the door on our familiar one flex two apartment was sad and painful in an unexpected way. Aunt Colleen picked us up in her old station wagon, we brought only our clothes and whatever books we could carry. The drive was long enough that it was easy for Aunt Colleen to get distracted. No one saw the bumper come across the divider until it was through the windshield, embedding itself in my chest.

No one tells you how sad it is to hear your own mother wail as the life leaves your body. No mother should have to bury her daughter. No daughter should die in her mother's arms.

"Your family sounds amazing." Siobhan smiled sadly.
"I miss them," Oona smiled sadly back, "I wish I had savored it more when my mama was fixing my hair."

CHAPTER 4

Seren

Having refreshed everyone's tea, allowing everyone's emotions to reset, Seren steeled herself when it was her turn to share the story of her life and death.

"Mine's a bit boring I'm afraid," the north of England carrying her voice as she began.

Growing up in a loving home, raised by loving parents who worked hard and loved harder, had its advantages. Having three siblings brings a built in ability to problem solve, honor oneself while still making room for other opinions and sharing the last bit of mash during Sunday roast. Oh there was so much love, it nearly blinded me to my differences.

The body I was born into did not belong to me, not really. It was a fine body, healthy, well fed, nary a bump or lump to be critiqued, even by judgmental church ladies. But it was a male body, my spirit was not and has never been that of man.

And so, just as silently as I had arrived in the world did I carry that burden to the grave.

Oh the life was good, it was great actually. Married my childhood sweetheart Millie and had as many children as I had siblings. They had arrived within five years of our nuptials which were announced in front of family and friends by our twenty two year old selves, when we were hardly as old as the new century itself.

The world had gone broke. Madness and hunger pushed too many to their brink and over the edge of their existence.

Yet, Millie and I remained happy. As happy as a couple can be when one half cannot truly be who they are. The smiles were real, the joy was real, the love was real. But I was not real. The wives of our friends counted Millie lucky to have such a present, equal partner in life. Many of those ladies spoke disparagingly of their husbands often at tea time; resentment is loud no matter when you sit in a house.

School was something I enjoyed so much I decided to become a teacher. Teachers have always been highly regarded where I am from thus, treated and paid well. Shaping young minds is something not to be taken lightly. Depending on the year, it was English or Humanities I taught to my secondary school students. And so it went for nearly sixty years.

Children recovered from scraped knees, bruised egos and broken hearts to become kind, happy adults with spouses and children of their own. Millie loved being a grandmother even more than she had loved being a mother. Delight may have been her most constant state, even through war, which I had only managed not to get pulled into by virtue of the day I was born. War tears everything asunder, whether you join them or not. New ways to destroy are invented, elaborated upon and executed even if most of the world does not want them.

Millie held my hand as my life slipped away, one of few times she'd cried. It seems a shame to lose sunshine altogether on account of just a bit of rain.

"Millie never suspected anything?"
"I played my part well," Seren replied sadly.
"It sounds like a lovely existence despite that," I replied.

Seren nodded, stirring more honey into her tea.

CHAPTER 5

Siobhan

My death was so recent it felt odd sharing it, as though I hadn't earned it, hadn't been dead long enough to have a tale to tell. Deep breath, no eye contact, here we go...

My long locks, a fuse igniting my scalp, were gone before I could really lament their loss. Some of my dress had melted onto my skin, smoking while it burned away. I tried to recall the way the sea spray felt on my face when I stole from my hammock in the middle of the night to stare at the stars. The thought of the cool night breeze pulling my black hair free of its braids as it passed from one end of the ship to the other, filling the sails with a gentle sigh, coaxing them along the journey.

My family lost everything we had, which wasn't much to begin with, so Father determined it better to leave our debts behind us and start over. Where he found the man who captained our journey remains a mystery, we found out in short order he was not adept at navigating which resulted in us landing on a very different island than planned. The coast I was raised on was colder than that we had crash landed upon. The people here were different. Kind but not artificially nice, sturdy, and watchful. They understood nature similarly to Druids from my bed time stories.

Wretching from the pain and the stench, hands pulling at nails that kept me where I stood. The stories told about burning at the stake never mention emesis. All the witches die beautiful and still whole, they are cut down by a forlorn lover and just cannot be revived, but they are still beautiful.

There was nothing beautiful about the grotesque creature I'd been twisted into by flames. Any strength left in my soul I used to imagine being anywhere but on rough beach rocks searing from the outside in.

It was a trick the Maori taught, using one's will to bend surroundings to oneself; I usually did it in the middle of winter when it was freezing and missed the sticky summer air frizzing my hair to embarrassing fullness or, in the middle of summer when the heat was just too much and I wished to feel snowflakes melt on too dry lips and sun kissed cheeks.

My heart began to beat an unsteady rhythm, my throat became uncomfortably dry, ribs started to crack and the pain of it all combined with the weight of my rapidly dissipating body, brought me to my knees. My heart stopped entirely, lungs could no longer inflate with the clean air I was so desperately trying to fill them with, all that occurred was sputtered gasps. Salty oceans and pleasant breezes abandoned me and my body began to burn in earnest; heart caught fire sending the spark through my veins with such speed muscles and nerves could have been a dry forest floor. Yesterday's breakfast baked to exposed ribs, my eyes had long since boiled to a puddle thus, sparing me the disgusted and piteous faces of those who had stayed to watch.

When I was finally able to meet their gaze, my cohort's tears streamed freely down their cheeks, falling into the hollows where skin once stretched.

"I'll never understand why some men sacrifice us for their own ends," Dwyn said.

"That's what happens when you mess with magic you don't understand," Oona chastised.

"Hear, hear," Seren raised her tea cup. Our resultant laughter replaced the silence that threatened to deflate our afternoon.

CHAPTER 6

The Dullahan

It was finally time to meet one of my would-be drivers. Some creatures arrive exactly as they are, some are plucked from Elsewhere by deities who deem them worthy, The Dullahan are the latter. They ride along the breeze on silver oak leaves, blowing across different planes, across time. Once a century, by Elsewhere measure, as Summer turns to Autumn, Arawn plucks a passing leaf, plunges it into the peat at Cliodhna's bog and by Winter Solstice a new Dullahan is added to the team.

When collecting folks from one plane and ushering them to the next, Banshee ride in Coiste Bodhar or Death Coach, helmed by none other than a headless horseman or more formally, and preferred, Dullahan. Our official tomes indicate The Dullahan remove their own heads in order to remain unbiased in the company of death. Legend would have you believe they are relieved of their heads as punishment and by way of control. Misdirection is the bedfellow of mystery, The Dullahan are experts in both.

Oona waited beside me at the stones in the bog where we met The Dullahan.

"I'll be back after the tour, these Sleepy Hollow fuckers still freak me out," a shiver visibly made it's way down Oona's spine.

Fog hung heavy in the air, mist trailing along the ground. They arrived so silently had I not been on the lookout for them, it would have been startling. As described, The Dullahan sat atop the coach, his head tucked in firmly on the bench seat next to him. Dressed in a black three piece suit, violet pocket square neatly folded , silver watch tucked into his waist coat. The coach he drove was massive, ornate and also, dressed for a funeral. As was the horse who pulled the carriage itself.

Approaching as slowly as possible lest excitement betray me, the horse leaned his muzzle into my hand as I made to pet it. Lost entirely in the presence of such a majestic animal, I'd missed entirely The Dullahan replacing his head on his shoulders.

"Hello," a deep voice boomed across the peat.
"If I weren't already dead you'd have frightened me to it," came out at nearly a wail.
"Apologies," he laughed, "I do so enjoy a jump scare. My name's Mike."

"What kind of name is that, now?"

"The kind Arawn gave me."

Cliodhna is Queen of the Banshee, Arawn rules the Otherworld. They afford each other an easy peace, an understanding only Gods of Death could have. What Cliodhna got up to in her daily life was largely turned a blind eye to, Arawn led a happy existence given his realm was perpetually an object of speculation. Some religions will tell you there are endless levels with varying degrees of torture. Arawn being the Afterlife of the Party was closer to the truth.

"Well then, Mike," I cleared my throat, "show me around the place."

Taking my hand, he led me around the carriage, describing various parts as we went. I recall none of the makings of a carriage. The assumption that they are black likely comes from the association with death overall however, Cothe de Bauer are the deepest purple. Easy mix up.

"I must say," Mike opened the carriage door, "you're taking this all in quite well."

"Oh," I huffed, stepping inside, "have you had averse reactions?"

"Not averse, no," he chuckled, "Oona let loose a few expletives on our first meeting, before being dragged back by Seren."

"What is this material," I interrupted, completely fixated on the bench seat fabric.

"Seats are velvet, wallpaper is mermaid tail, it's more chainmail in nature than fish scales as one would assume," pausing to consider and to take a breath, "our horses live as long as we do."

"How do you come about the mermaid tale?"

"These carriages are ancient," he said, holding out a hand to help me down, "and The Fair Folk are quite cruel."

"I have yet to experience their cruelty first hand," I confessed.

"I pray you never do."

Pleasantries out of the way, Mike took me for a drive around the block as they say. It is the one and only time they share the driver's seat, eases you into the journey and gives you a different perspective. We started slowly, staving off potentially losing one's breakfast though, brisk enough to stir a breeze in our wake and for the horse to enjoy the movement.

"We typically have four horses pulling the carriage, since today is training, you just get Clover here," he smiled broadly.

"Why four?"

"As you'd imagine, crossing time and planes of existence is taxing work," pulling the reins, Clover guided us around a tree stump, "such things are better done together."

"I may come to regret this but, how does one care for Otherworldly horses?"

"As well as they deserve. All the barmbrack and black and white pudding they can eat, as well as apples of course. They are our constant companions so we treat them as well as ourselves."

"What, no boiled bacon and cabbage?"

"That would be terribly offensive to Arawn," he said flatly, taking his eyes off the pathway for the only time during our journey.

"Apologies, I did not know."

"Arawn has many companions, some of which are Boar, and good luck to anyone who tries to hunt or eat them."

"Boar is an interesting companion choice."

"Ah he has many, he prefers them though," reining Clover in again, we began our journey back.

"Have you ever collected a soul who did not want to be collected?"

It was my greatest fear and one I had yet to ask of my Curse.

"Oh yes."

"How did you manage it?"

Mike was silent for what felt like a very long time.

"Ever tried to bathe a cat?"

I shook my head no.

"They scratch, bite and scream the whole time until, eventually, they gouge your eye out or give in to the inevitable."

"Well then, I am glad to see you've still got both eyes."

We completed the rest of our journey in an easy silence. I hoped Mike would always be my driver or at least that the others were equally kind and I really wanted to see Clover again.

"Realta said we may meet again when we get a call, thank you for showing me around," a curtsy and a nod my salutation, a hop and a squelch his.

CHAPTER 7

First Watch

The sound of gently tinkling bells pulled me from dreaming, I had been delighted to discover I still dreamed here. Oona sat at the end of my bed, tapping gently to make sure I was awake. Seeing her in her bonnet every morning felt very familiar and made me smile every time, seeing her mid sleep cycle was a bit jarring.

"We got a call," she whispered, "let's get dressed as quickly as we can."

Off she went with me following closely. Getting ready for work was very new for me, having only done chores before as women did not work during the time I was alive. Checking each other's braids and that we were dressed well enough, one cannot look shabby when collecting a soul, we were off to the bog to meet our Dullahan.

My worries eased a bit once I saw Clover leading the carriage around the corner. She carried herself proudly among the other three. Oona barely disguised her discomfort. Mike popped his head on before hopping down, opened the carriage door and helped us inside. He tapped the door after it closed to make sure it was secured.

"This should be an easy one," Oona began, reading from a scroll Realta had given her, "We are heading to a farm in the 1800's, farmer was gored by a bull, and the family brought him into the barn. He should be passed by the time we arrive."

"What is his name?"

"William Smyth, aged thirty four."

"Family?"

"Wife, four kids with another on the way."

"What's the wife's name?"

"Maureen."

"Thirty four," I shook my head, "that's a good long run."

"Sometimes I forget," Oona chuckled, "that you are from a vastly different time. People were living for a century during my lifetime."

"Centuries? How?"

"Medicine, standards of living and education evolved quite a bit from your time to mine though, nothing is ever perfect."

"How are you doing seeing Mike?"

"I've come a long way since my vomit fertilized the bog every single call," she shook her head, "maybe I'll be able to look them in the eye soon."

"I'll admit, at first glance they are offputting" I assured her, "they've never scared me though."

"Ichabod may have been well after you but, Sleepy Hollow is a very real and very spooky place. My family visited once but I was so affected by the ghastly things there that we never went back."

"More ghastly than being driven in a death coach pulled by Otherworldly horses, led by a headless man?"

"There were actual terrors in the schoolhouse we visited. Ghosts of people who looked like me and had endured unspeakable things."

"Oh," my breath caught in my throat, "I am so sorry, Oona."

"I think we're here," she responded flatly.

Sure enough, the carriage was slowing down. We pulled our masks up over our mouths as we came to a halt. The carriage door swung open on its own and Oona began a low keen as we stepped down to greet our charge. Her voice grew louder, each step carrying us closer to the barn. The children were young, red eyed from crying and had their hands over their ears when they finally came into view.

Oona's wailing had reached peak pitch and volume, the soul of the departed along with it. He stood up, leaving his body behind, dusted himself off and smiled broadly as he turned to meet us. Oona nodded at his wife, hoping she understood her late husband was in good hands, she nodded in answer.

Oona stopped her keening once we were all securely in the carriage, William and herself sharing the bench across from me.

"Wife never wanted that bull," he chuckled, "was always worried he'd trample the kids. Jokes on me I suppose."

"Bulls are temperamental creatures, you won't be the last to meet their end by way of horn," I assured him.

"So which place am I headed then? Upstairs or down?"

"We aren't privy to that," Oona said, "both options suit well enough for an Afterlife. The heat of one has been greatly exaggerated."

"Ah too bad that, I was hoping to warm my bones at least."

The journey back was swift, Mike pulled us to a stop once more just outside a large, ornate gate. Just beyond the gate the sun was rising over a dewy meadow from which wafted a heady scent of honey and clover.

"It smells different for everyone," Mike said just behind me, "whatever home smells like to you, that is how you'll be greeted."

"Does everyone have their own little slice or, how does that work?"

"In a way, yes."

"Move," Oona snipped at Mike who, of course, obliged.

"Ah now, this looks lovely," William smiled.

Oona handed Mike a sheaf of paper, we are required to record time of death, collection and emotional state along with our names and signatures to make things official. After a once over determining it satisfied protocol, he walked William through the gate leaving us to wait in the carriage.

"What do they hear while we're wailing," only just realizing I hadn't been called in the same way we collect others.

Oona smiled at the question, "they hear the first song they heard in life."

"It's different for everyone then?"

Oona nodded, keeping an eye on the gate for Mike's return.

"What would yours have been?"

Without hesitation Oona replied "a song by Ms Flack," she said and began humming the gentle tune.

If every collection went this way, I may actually have some fun after all.

CHAPTER 8

Weights and Measures

I had been with my Curse long enough to have gone on a handful of collections with each of them, save Realta. Since she was in charge of us, Realta was responsible for administration and oversight, to include attending meetings when necessary so collection was not her purview. As it was, my review was due so, in Realta's office I found myself. It was much like our rooms; cozy, well furnished, no shortage of tea.

"How have you found things so far," she asked while pouring tea for each of us.

"Great," I began, stirring honey into my English Breakfast, "my Curse is lovely and collecting seems very straightforward."

"But," Realta raised a brow, interpreting my tone correctly.

"Its just that, well," taking a breath to steady my nerves, "I was raised with certain ideas about death and I'm wondering how suicides are dealt with?"

"How do you mean?"

"Well," I hesitated, "do we take them somewhere else?"

"Ah," Realta nodded, finishing her sip, "we collect, we do not judge."

"Hell is not real?"

"Nor is Heaven. Religion is human made, the Gods they create them after in an effort to control human behaviors is nowhere near what the Gods themselves want."

"What do the gods want then?"

"They want for nothing," Realta stirred more tea and cream into her cup, "they create, they care take, they make love, they make war with each other. They may get bored and choose to visit a human realm for a time but, they don't interfere with human affairs, they think little of them if they think of them at all, until it suits them. Humans forget that they themselves are the fabric of the universe, and while they may not have god-like power, they are still important."

"What about people who commit crimes or injustices against others? What about Angels and Demons?"

"There are Infernal beings and Otherworldly beings. As above, so below and all that, there must be a balance to things."

Seren interrupted just then to let them know they'd received a call. Realta thanked her and let her know she and I would take it. Nerves bubbled up in my stomach as I followed Realta to The Bog.

"You wondered about suicide," Realta said, reading the details on our journey, "we're on our way to one now. Forty-two year old Vincent Bradley, divorced, no children."

The Dullahan who drove us tonight was called Sean, he was only the fourth Dullahan I'd met. Sean was serious and seemed indifferent to the team of horses who pulled his carriage. Realta assured me he was very good at what he did, even if he was more stoic than Mike.

Realta began keening as we slowed down, pulling her mask on only when we stopped, keening louder as we exited the Death Coach.

We arrived in Casper, Wyoming in 2020. There was a record scratching away and several scented candles burning low, the windows in the first floor apartment had been thrown open so it was deathly cold. He was sitting up looking around himself when he noticed we were there. The violent method he used to end his existence left most of his blood and half his brain on the wall behind him.

"The whole world shut down," he said, "the whole world shut down and I was forgotten."

Realta wailed ever louder. Vincent stood up, looking down at his lifeless body as he did.

"Who are you," he shuddered, "why are you here?"

Realta's keen steadied, holding an impossible note.

"I think I made a mistake."

"Sean we've got a runner," I shouted as the spirit of Vincent Bradley turned to run.

No sooner had the last word left my lips did Sean leap from the driver's seat to the back of the lead horse in his team, pulling his own head from his neck as he did. Vincent made it a few feet before he was taken down by Sean's head like a pin in a game of bowling. Mike had described reluctant souls being collected, how shame choked sense from their minds.

Vincent struggled the whole way back and into the carriage before giving into death entirely; Sean remained unfazed throughout the incident. Vincent cried our entire journey back, as Sean dragged him through the gate, the noise of his lamentation stopped only after he passed into whatever lay beyond.

"He's making it worse than it is," Realta explained as we watched, "Arawn will have an audience with him, determine his readiness to go back and Vincent will wait until it's time or spend the rest of his afterward there, in whichever version of The Otherworld is suitable for him."

"That's it," shock inflecting my tone.

"That's it," Realta nodded, "no fire, no torture aside from that which Vincent puts himself through. If he forgives himself he may even find time for a new hobby."

"Hobby," I chuckled at the thought.
"Maybe basket weaving is still en vogue."

Wailer of the Keen

Your presence is formally requested
by Their Royal Majesty's of
Bansalee and their court, on the
occasion of The Passing of the
Crown Kindly make yourself
available at moonrise on Samhain
two-thousand twenty-three. Included
please find one oak leaf, plucked on
the third day of the waxing moon
during Beltane, as your passage
between planes.

Yours sincerely,
Lady of the quills of the realm of Bansalee

CHAPTER 9

Ascent

My Curse helped me prepare for the coronation the only way any of us knew how: laughing along as we stitched together the perfect image of distinguished Banshee. They honored me with their unique gifts; Oona twisted my hair into the most elaborate braids I'd ever had. Dwyn painted my face, Seren ensured my skirts were appropriately full and, Realta lent me a ring of deep amethyst set in silver.

When they were satisfied that I would represent us well, they walked me to my departure point, kissed my cheeks and made me promise to tell them everything upon my return.

The sensation of dying resets your expectations for all others that follow so, the sudden weightlessness and near break neck speed that carried me between planes was nothing in comparison. The Dullahan would be very proud of my arriving with nary a hair out of place.

The moon had fully risen by the time the centuries old oak tree greeted me on the side of the mountain. Known colloquially as Peppersauce Canyon, the Native tribes this land belonged to had certainly called it something more worthy of its beauty.

There would likely be no humans present so the mask typically worn was eschewed, breathing free air for the first time in a long time. A dark haired sprite peeked around the trunk of a very big tree, giggling when he spied me looking his way, motioning for silence. Airioch, Teagan's Feandragoon, hovered nearby keeping a close watch on her charge.

"Ready or not, here I come," a deep voice announced their game. To my surprise, the King of Bansalee appeared over the hill, a silver crown set with fire opals, emeralds and sapphires set atop his dark wavy locks. Wearing his finest was never an option, especially not on his retirement day.

His broad smile lit up by mischief and moonlight eased any nerves I once had, that was his gift and was part of what made him a good leader. As all good grandfathers do, he pretended to be blind and deaf to his grandson, letting himself be caught instead. Which isn't the game but is always how the game goes with sprites.

"Edmond, this is Siobhan," he introduced them, Edmond sitting on his hip.
"We've met already," Edmond giggled.

"Indeed we have," I agreed, "he graciously let me in on his hiding spot."

"It's good to see you," King Patrick took my bony hand in his, kissing the back of it as I courtseyed.

"You honor me sir," I responded earnestly.

"The honor is ours, I'm sure," he turned so we could walk the short way to the grove together.

"How is our heir feeling?"

"Oh," he shook his head, "you know Teagan. She makes sure everything is just so. My wife has been absolutely bent to her will, as usual. I think Rette is having a harder time, if I'm honest."

"Oh?"

"He struggles being who he is at times, as do we all."

"That is the most common experience for any creature."

Edmond chatted away as we strolled, regaling me with the goings on between cousins and siblings. He was Teagan's second child, her first with her new paramour, Edmond reminded me very much of his father, who is a very good man.

Being among the last to arrive has its benefits, for instance your seat is very obvious and everyone else has had at least one intoxicant so my visage was less shocking than it otherwise would be. Arawn and his wife were already there, nodding acknowledgment when our eyes met, as were all of Teagan's family and friends. The new paramour in question was running a bit behind, work matters as I understood it.

Teagan was in her dressing tent with her mother and Meagan, putting the finishing touches on the evening as was their tradition. Seeing so many Fair Folk in one place would usually be cause for concern but tonight was a happy exception. Smoothing my garments out of habit, Trystan had finally arrived dressed as smartly as anything, and everyone took their place.

Instrumental music began playing quietly, indicating everyone should take their seat. Teagan floated down from the canopy of leaves on gossamer feather wings that partially obscured the full moon light. Crownless hair upswept in a vision of scarlet perfection, she traded her default all black everything for deep emerald, accessorized with silver jewelry and for the first time in all the years Siobhan had known her, she was barefoot.

Never one to hide her emotion, she glided as slowly as possible toward the altar where her father, The King, waited to pass his well wrought torch, glee flushing her cheeks, broadening her smile, twitching through her wings.

"We have always done things a little differently here," King Patrick began the moment his daughter had settled before him, "tonight will be no exception."

He paused for breath and to take his heir's left hand in his right, energetically receiving and giving, smiling as he began again.

"You have helped me become the King I am as much as anyone else and in some ways more than anyone else ever could by holding up a mirror as my own duplicate. When choosing to build anew instead of continuing to uphold an ineffective model of ruling, I knew it was not for the faint of heart, luckily I don't scare easily and I happen to have been blessed with the most dedicated partner. Our Queen," he nodded at Teagan's mother sitting front row, tears streaming from her dark eyes down perfectly sculpted cheekbones, "believed in me when I did not believe in myself, when all seemed lost and I determined to wallow in hardship. Nevertheless, we persisted and now, what seems many lifetimes later, it is time for youth to carry our kingdom forward. Mo anam, Mo chroi, Teagan Inez Patrick McCarthy, do you swear to uphold the values established for The Kingdom of Bansalee and the people you are bound to protect?"

"I swear," Teagan responded seriously.

"Can you recite those values before me and the people you hold most dear?"

"I swear to honor the land borrowed from nature and the peoples who came before us, leaving it better that we found it. I swear to honor the least of us, keep humble the greatest of us, encourage diplomacy above all, and enact war on their behalf only as a last resort. I swear to honor the Goddess, The Oracle and The Mother, as they honor me with the gifts of life, intuition and purpose."

Neither her gaze nor her voice wavered, as she has always been and always will be unwavering, her spirit made of the strongest fabric of the universe, never frayed nor faltered. Then the party began in earnest.

The Patricks were renowned for their soiree's, a coronation was cause for pulling out whatever stops they previously enacted for other parties. As always, Jack catered. He was the only one Teagan trusted to serve without consulting a menu, carte blanche the foundation of their friendship. Jacks Bistro signature brussel sprout chips with poppy seed dressing were of course a feature, as was the endless supply of pomegranate mead, various soups, dips and meats. Coronation Cakes were set out after everything else, lemon lavender, spumoni and, plain vanilla for those who prefer that sort of thing.

I'd never said Slainte so much in my life or death and was so well joyed by the time I left, I could hardly decipher the rising sun from the mirth lighting up the sky.

CHAPTER 10

Cursed

The journey home as swift as the journey there though, my heart felt more full than ever. Witnessing our friends is one of the greatest gifts we can give each other, witnessing a steadfast, fair minded leader take a throne made just for her felt like a mighty gift indeed. Queen Teagan would be a welcome addition to a Curse someday though what her afterward held was up to the Gods.

My curse was waiting for me, tea and scones at the ready. Shucking my formal wear, dressing for a morning in, I joined them near the fire roaring for ambience only. Oona in her bonnet, Dwyn's untidy braid, Seren's perfectly messy bun accompanied by their bright smiles and sleepy morning musings had become the start of my days without me noticing. At that moment, sipping and spilling tea, I never wanted it to end, never wanted any other beginning to my days. For the first time I was home, truly home which, a great surprise for me, is a Curse.

CHAPTER 11

Realta

Unlike my beloved Curse, I have always been as we are, I was not made Banshee, I *am* Banshee. There are few of us left, casualties of wars between quick to anger deities. We do not belong to the world, we are not of the world, we are merely a thread in the vastness of the tapestry called Bith.

Our Queen Cliodhna, the goddess of love and beauty, plucked us from the stars in the sea and so, we are. As ruthless as she is beautiful, she laments the loss of each Banshee with the loveliest keening ever wailed. For once a Banshee is gone from the hereafter, she is gone forever.

Ushering the departed from one plane to the next is quite thankless though fulfilling none the less. Keeping a Curse helps pass the time, takes the sting out of an Afterlife of service. Befriending The Dullahan makes the bumpier transports less so.

Someday a Banshee will come for you and when she does, I hope you greet her like a friend and think fondly of her song across all your lifetimes.

Acknowledgements

Much like Siobhan, I wouldn't get very far without my friends and the food wouldn't be nearly as good. To begin with my dear friend, poet, Dungeon Master extraordinaire and cover artist, Ben Buller, was among the first to encourage my writing and is finally no longer a fan club of one. You can find his artwork @20sidedstudios on Instagram. My critique partner helped with editing, for which I am endlessly grateful (and so are you) go buy all the things Peter Baker writes, thank me later. Jack, we exist in each others universes in every life time, thank you for seeing me and, cheers to thirteen years. Kim, Kimmy, Kimbearly, you're the best thing I've found on the internet so far. Allison, Cara, JB and Trish, I appreciate you all so much, I am so glad we decided to take a chance on each other in that little coffee shop that day and cannot wait to see what we do next.

*T Squared
Photography*

Maggie was born and raised in Southern Arizona, loves travel, tacos, supporting Womens Wrongs and hopes you'll tell your cat pspsps. Lately she has been pouring into the Indie Author community via Tucson Author Alliance and perfecting her pumpkin roll recipe. Follow her on socials @maggs_the_rad_writes, don't make it weird.

www.ingramcontent.com/pod-product-compliance
Lightning Source LLC
Chambersburg PA
CBHW030012010826

48973CB00009B/2777